This book belongs to:

_____

This paperback edition published in 2011 by Andersen Press Ltd.
Published in Australia by Random House Australia Pty.,
Level 3, 100 Pacific Highway, North Sydney, NSW 2060.
First published in Great Britain in 1971 by Blackie & Son Limited.
Text copyright © John Yeoman, 1971
Illustration copyright © Quentin Blake, 1971
The rights of John Yeoman and Quentin Blake to be identified as the
author and illustrator of this work have been asserted by them in
accordance with the Copyright, Designs and Patents Act, 1988.
All rights reserved.
Colour separated in Switzerland by Photolitho AG, Zürich.
Printed in China.
Quentin Blake has used watercolour, pen and ink in this book.

10   9   8   7   6   5   4   3   2   1

British Library Cataloguing in Publication Data available.
Trade ISBN 978 1 84939 308 9
Special Sales ISBN 978 1 78344 239 3

This book has been printed on acid-free paper

John Yeoman & Quentin Blake

Sixes and Sevens

ANDERSEN PRESS

Early one morning Barnaby's mother saw him off on his raft. "Don't forget to stop at each village on the way to Limber Lea," she said, "in case anyone wants you to take anything for them."

Barnaby picked up his pole and called out, "I shan't forget."

"And remember to look in your big box if you have any difficulties," shouted his mother, as he set off.

1

First he stopped at Harmer's Landing and was met by Abigail Crumb:

"I've just one kitten to send," she said,
"As quiet as quiet can be.
She'll sleep for hours on end," she said,
"From here to Limber Lea."

"No difficulties so far," said Barnaby.
"Perhaps I shall have an easy journey to Limber Lea."

2

Next he stopped at Long-Acre Bottom
and was met by Honor Blaskett:

"I've just two mice, the dears," she said,
"As quiet as quiet can be.
But Kitty will chew their ears," she said,
"From here to Limber Lea."

So Barnaby looked in his big box
to see what he could see,
and he pulled out a sock.
"The kitten can stay in the sock from
here to Limber Lea," he said,
"and then I won't have any difficulties."

3

Next he stopped at Parson's Barrow
and was met by Felicity Parfitt:

"Three schoolmistresses, stiff as twigs,"
she said,
"As quiet as quiet can be.
But the mice will get in their wigs,"
she said,
"From here to Limber Lea."

So Barnaby looked in his big box
to see what he could see,
and pulled out a jam jar.
"The mice can stay in the jam jar from
here to Limber Lea," he said,
"and then I won't have any difficulties."

Next he stopped at Stukey Ford
and was met by Samantha Heydey:

"Four schoolboys, clean and bright,"
she said,
"As quiet as quiet can be.
But the teachers will fill them with
fright," she said,
"From here to Limber Lea."

So Barnaby looked in his big box
to see what he could see,
and he pulled out some knitting needles
and some balls of wool.
"The schoolmistresses can knit from here
to Limber Lea," he said,
"and then I won't have any difficulties."

5

Next he stopped at Couchgrass
Common and was met by Mercy Lord:

"Five monkeys, sharp as nails,"
she said,
"As quiet as quiet can be.
But the boys will tug at their tails,"
she said,
"From here to Limber Lea."

So Barnaby looked in his big box
to see what he could see,
and he pulled out some paints and paper.
"The boys can do some painting
from here to Limber Lea," he said,
"and then I won't have any difficulties."

6

Next he stopped at Reuben's Lock
and was met by Susannah Rebeck:

"Six parrots who all can speak,"
she said,
"As quiet as quiet can be.
But the monkeys will make them shriek,"
she said,
"From here to Limber Lea."

So Barnaby looked in his big box
to see what he could see,
and he pulled out a large wooden cage.
"The monkeys can stay in the cage
from here to Limber Lea," he said,
"and then I won't have any difficulties."

7

Next he stopped at Merryweather
Mill and was met by Martha Kirk:

"Seven dogs (I couldn't find more),"
she said,
"As quiet as quiet can be.
But the parrots will peck them sore,"
she said,
"From here to Limber Lea."

So Barnaby looked in his big box
to see what he could see,
and he pulled out a large bird-stand.
"The parrots can perch on the stand
from here to Limber Lea," he said,
"and then I won't have any difficulties."

8

Next he stopped at Pollard's Weir
and was met by Deborah Winnow:

"Eight snakes, some slender, some stout,"
she said,
"As quiet as quiet can be.
But the dogs will shake them about,"
she said,
"From here to Limber Lea."

So Barnaby looked in his big box
to see what he could see,
and he pulled out some beautiful leads.
"The dogs can stay on the leads from
here to Limber Lea," he said,
"and then I won't have any difficulties."

9

Next he stopped at Saltmarsh Flats
and was met by Eliza Distaff:

"Nine frogs, green, black, and brown,"
she said,
"As quiet as quiet can be.
But the snakes will gulp them down,"
she said,
"From here to Limber Lea."

So Barnaby looked in his big box
to see what he could see,
and he pulled out a lot of drainpipes.
"The snakes can stay in the drainpipes
from here to Limber Lea," he said,
"and then I won't have any difficulties."

Next he stopped at Sandy Elbow
and was met by Dorothea Gurdon:

"Ten grasshoppers, bright and gay,"
she said,
"As quiet as quiet can be.
But the frogs will chase them away,"
she said,
"From here to Limber Lea."

So Barnaby looked in his big box
to see what he could see,
and he pulled out an enormous
goldfish bowl, full of water.
"The frogs can stay in the bowl from
here to Limber Lea," he said,
"and then I won't have any difficulties."

So Barnaby got his raft to Limber Lea safely, and there waiting for him were ten cheerful people who had come to collect their

1

one kitten

2

two mice

3

three schoolmistresses

4 four schoolboys

5 five monkeys

6

six parrots

7

seven dogs

8

eight snakes

9

nine frogs

10

and ten grasshoppers.

And then Barnaby drifted all the way back home, pleased with his good day's work.

Also illustrated by Quentin Blake:

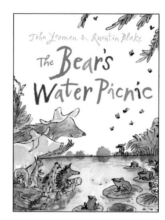